The Safari Children's Books
on Good Behavior

Maxi the Monkey Learns Why Going to Bed Early is Important

by
Cressida Elias

Illustrated by Carriel Ann Santos

Maxi was a kind little monkey. He lived in a beautiful treehouse in the African rainforest.

He liked to help his parents because he loved being busy! It also made his parents very happy. And when they smiled it made him smile too.

He would hunt with them for food, help around the treehouse and tidy his bedroom every day!

His parents were very pleased with him. However, one evening when it was bedtime and his parents were very tired after a long day hunting for food, Maxi started to 'monkey' around.

When his Mother called out 'Bedtime!' Maxi did not go to bed.

In fact he started to do somersaults, swing on branches, eat bananas and do ANYTHING but go to bed!

'No Mum, I want to play some more, I'm not tired yet,' he cried out.

'But Maxi, its late, you have had your play time,' said his Mother.

'All our monkey friends are already in bed. It's important to get lots of sleep so you have energy when we get up in the morning,' continued his Mother.

Maxi's Mother had a good idea.

'I know, let's read a little story and you will soon feel like sleeping' she said.

But Maxi didn't listen. He just wanted to play.

His parents climbed into their bed and waited for Maxi to do the same.

Eventually, when it was very dark indeed, Maxi climbed up the tree and got into his bed.

'It's very late now. I just hope we are not too tired to hunt for food tomorrow!' said his Father.

The morning arrived very quickly and the sun shone brightly through the leaves on the trees.

All the other monkeys in other trees jumped out of bed and scrambled down to start their day.

But Maxi and his parents yawned and found it hard to get out of bed! They felt tired as well as a little grumpy.

Maxi curled up again and wondered if he could just stay at home that day!

But they all had to get up and go looking for fresh fruit and nuts.

It was very hard to work that day. They were too tired to gather lots of food and Maxi was even too tired to play with the other monkey kids.

Maxi didn't have much fun.

When the sun started to set they came home, weary-eyed and ready for bed.

'I'm going to bed right away!' said Maxi with a rather large yawn. 'I want to have lots of energy tomorrow so I can have fun when I work and even *more* fun when I play!'

His Mother smiled 'Maxi, I think that is a very good idea... well done for thinking of it' she added.

Maxi brushed his teeth, kissed his Mum and Dad goodnight and jumped into bed.

And straight away he fell fast asleep, dreaming of fresh green leaves and bananas.

Next morning as soon as the sun rose, Maxi sat up. He rubbed his eyes. It looked like it was going to be another hot, sunny day.

'What a beautiful day!' he said out loud. And he felt great. He slid down the tree and had his breakfast his Mother had prepared. It was fresh green leaves and bananas! Just what I love, he thought.

His Mum and Dad smiled. What a bright young monkey he is this morning!

Maxi looked back at his Mum and Dad ...and they smiled back.

Going to bed early must have pleased them. And it certainly did!

They awarded him a big golden star badge.

It said "Good Little Monkey". He loved it!

From then on Maxi decided he would *always* go to bed on time.

That way, he would'nt be tired the next day and he would *always* be able to wear his 'Good Little Monkey' badge with pride!

But most important of all, his parents would always smile at him

And when they smiled, he smiled and the world was a better place!

The End

Safari Children's Books on Good Behavior

www.safarichildrensbooks.com

Printed in Great Britain
by Amazon.co.uk, Ltd.,
Marston Gate.